NO! NO! WORD BIRD

by Jane Belk Moncure

illustrated by Linda Sommers Hohag

THE CHILD'S WORLD

ELGIN, ILLINOIS 60120

Distributed by Childrens Press, 1224 West Van Buren Street, Chicago, Illinois 60607.

Library of Congress Cataloging in Publication Data

Moncure, Jane Belk.
    No! No! Word Bird.

    (Her Word Birds for early birds)
    SUMMARY: Word Bird presents such cautions as a stove
being hot, and keeping warm and dry on a winter day.
    [1. Birds—Fiction]   I. Hohag, Linda.   II. Title.
III. Series.
PZ7.M739No 1981   [E]   80-29491
ISBN 0-89565-161-0

NO! NO!
WORD BIRD

"No! No!
The stove is hot!"

"Hot! Yes, hot!"

"No! No!
The snow is cold!"

"Yes!
The snow is cold!"

"Come back!
The snow is cold!

"Get your cap,

your scarf,

and your boots!"

"No! No!
Come down!"

"Oh! Oh!"

"No! No! Take off

your cap

and your scarf

and your boots!

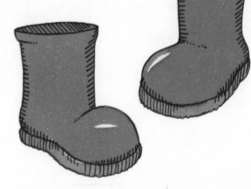

You are wet!"

"Yes, I am wet and cold!"

"Come here.
The fire is hot."

"The soup is hot."

"I am hot!
I am dry.
I am going out.
Bye - bye."

"No! No!
Come back!
The snow is cold!

"Get your cap

and your scarf

and your boots!"

"Hi!"

"Hi! Let's go for a ride!"

"No! No!
You will fall off!"

"Oh! Oh!"

"Let's skate!"

"Bye - bye."

"No! No!
Come back!"

"No! No!
Come back!"

"Good!
Word Bird is a
good bird!"

"Yes, Yes."

Can you read these words with  Word Bird?

stove

soup

hot

fire

cold

ride

cap

skate

scarf

no   yes

boots

bye-bye!